Amy Lauer

STUART·LITTLE ™

The Great Boat Race

D1472239

Based on the screenplay by
Gregory J. Brooker and M. Night Shyamalan

HarperTrophy®
A Division of HarperCollinsPublishers

COLUMBIA PICTURES PRESENTS A DOUGLAS WICK AND FRANKLIN/WATERMAN PRODUCTION A FILM BY ROB MINKOFF GEENA DAVIS "STUART LITTLE" HUGH LAURIE AND JONATHAN LIPNICKI CO-PRODUCER JASON CLARK MUSIC BY ALAN SILVESTRI EXECUTIVE PRODUCERS JEFF FRANKLIN AND STEVE WATERMAN BASED ON THE BOOK BY E.B. WHITE SCREENPLAY BY GREGORY J. BROOKER AND M. NIGHT SHYAMALAN PRODUCED BY DOUGLAS WICK DIRECTED BY ROB MINKOFF DISTRIBUTED THROUGH SONY PICTURES RELEASING IN CANADA: DISTRIBUTED THROUGH COLUMBIA TRISTAR FILMS OF CANADA

www.stuartlittle.com

COLUMBIA PICTURES

The Great Boat Race

© 1999 Columbia Pictures Industries, Inc. All Rights Reserved.

Adaptation by Kitty Richards

Illustrations by Carolyn Bracken

Harper Trophy® is a registered trademark of HarperCollins Publishers Inc.

Printed in the U.S.A. All Rights Reserved.

Library of Congress catalog card number: 99-62458

ISBN 0-06-444268-3

More than anything,
George Little wanted a little brother.
If he had a little brother
he could teach him to play ball, to wrestle,
and even how to spit.
They could play together all day long.

But when George met his new brother
he was very surprised. Stuart was just a mouse
And George didn't think he wanted
a mouse for a little brother.
What would they be able to do together?

Stuart was *really* little.
When he ate, he had to sit on a stack
of books to reach the table.

The only clothes his size
were from the toy department.
And Mrs. Little could lift him up with
one hand.

The Littles lived near the park.
Every year there was a sailboat race.
This year, George wanted to enter.
He had been building a boat in his
basement.
It was called the *Wasp*.

All the other kids' boats were from the store.
George didn't think his boat could win.
But Stuart knew better.
So, he got George to enter the race.
And the two of them finished the boat
just in time.

On the day of the race the Littles and
Stuart went to cheer for George.

A boy named Anton Gartran arrived.
His boat was called the *Lillian B. Womrath*.
"I'm glad you're here, George," he said.
"*Somebody* has to finish last."
Anton was not very nice at all.

It was almost time for the race to begin.
George and Mr. Little needed to lower
the *Wasp* into the water.
George asked Stuart to hold the boat's
remote control.
"Aye, aye, Captain!" said Stuart.

But the remote control was heavy—
too heavy for a little mouse—
and Stuart dropped it.
Crunch! A man in big boots stepped on it.
The remote control was ruined.
George was very upset.
Now he couldn't
even be in the race.

"On your mark, get set, go!"
shouted the race starter.
The horn blared and all the boats took off.
The starter pointed to the *Wasp*.
"Hey! Is that a mouse on that boat?"
George and the Littles pushed to the
front of the crowd.
"It's Stuart!" they cried.

Stuart was sailing!

But he was last—dead last.

Then he changed direction.

Soon the *Wasp* was catching up.

Anton saw what was happening.
So he steered his boat straight at the *Wasp*.
"Stuart, look out!" cried George.

Crash!

The *Womrath* slammed into the *Wasp*.

The boats got all tangled up.

Stuart ran up the mast to free the boats.

The *Womrath* sailed away.
Stuart lifted his sail and tied the line.
Then the *Wasp* began to pick up speed.
Soon the two boats were almost at the
finish line.

The *Womrath* was just ahead of the *Wasp*.
Just then, the *Womrath*'s sail tore in two.
It spun around
and headed straight for the *Wasp*!

The Littles all held their breath.
Would the two boats crash?
But Stuart slid down the sail
and grabbed the wheel.

The *Wasp* raced around the *Womrath* and across the finish line. Stuart was the winner! Everyone cheered— George the loudest of all.

"Who is that mouse?" someone asked.
"That's no mouse," George said proudly.
"That's my brother!"